POKÉMON

THE HAUNTED GYM

Adapted by Tracey West

Scholastic Inc.

New York   Toronto   London   Auckland   Sydney
Mexico City   New Delhi   Hong Kong   Buenos Aires

ISBN 0-439-42988-9

12 11 10 9 8   7/0

Printed in the U.S.A.
First Scholastic printing, September 2002

One day, Ash and his friends Misty and Brock came to a new town.

"*Pika!*" said Pikachu. The yellow Pokémon was happy to be in a new place.

"I need to find the Pokémon gym," Ash said. "I am ready for a Pokémon battle!"

Brock found the gym on a map. "Follow me," he said.

"Is this really the gym?" Misty asked.
"It looks spooky."

Then something scary happened.

The gym was on fire!

Hot flames burned all around them.
"Run!" yelled Ash.

Ash and his friends ran away from the flames.

"Oh no!" said Brock. "What should we do?"

Ash and Misty knew what to do.

They called on Totodile and Staryu, their Water Pokémon.

"Put out that fire!" Ash and Misty yelled.

Totodile and Staryu shot water at the fire.
But the flames would not go out!

Then Totodile got a funny look on its face. It jumped right into the flames! But Totodile was not hurt.

"The flames are not hot," Misty said.

"They are not real!" Ash cried.

Ash called on Noctowl, a Pokémon that can see through tricks like fake fire.

"Noctowl, use your Foresight!" Ash
yelled.

A red beam came out of Noctowl's
eyes. The beam shone on the flames.

It worked! Ash saw that the flames were not real. They were made by a group of Ghost Pokémon called Gastly!

The Gastly attacked Noctowl. Noctowl tackled the Gastly.

The Gastly vanished. But they came right back. And they had lots of Haunter with them!

"There are Ghost Pokémon all around us!" Misty cried.

Ash called on Pikachu. "Use your
Thundershock!"

But before Pikachu could attack, an
older boy came down the stairs.
    "Stop!"
he yelled.

A Ghost
Pokémon stood
next to the boy.
It was a Gengar.

The Gastly and Haunter seemed afraid of
Gengar. Then the boy waved his hand. The
Gastly and Haunter vanished into the
walls.

"Hello, I am Morty," the boy said. "I am the gym leader in this town. This is the old gym. Only Ghost Pokémon live here now."

While Morty talked, Togepi snuck away.

"Togepi, come back!" Misty yelled.

The little Pokémon ran through a small hole in the wall. Pikachu ran after Togepi.

Pikachu ran into the hole, too.

"How will we find them?" Misty asked.
"Gengar and the Ghost Pokémon
can help," Morty said. "They can look
for Togepi and Pikachu."

Outside the gym, Team Rocket was up to no good.

Jessie, James, and Meowth were looking for treasure.

But they did not find money or gold. They found . . .

"Togepi!" Jessie cried.

"Now that is a *real* treasure," said Meowth.

Pikachu ran up, but it was too late. Meowth grabbed Togepi.

"*Pika!*" Pikachu wanted to shock Team Rocket.

"If you zap us, you will zap Togepi, too," Meowth warned.

Pikachu could not fight back. Now Team Rocket had Pikachu, too!

A Gastly saw the whole thing. It flew back to Morty and told him what had happened.

Team Rocket started to run. Pikachu and
Togepi could not get away!

Morty's Gengar flew very fast. It used its long tongue to trip Team Rocket.

Ash and his friends ran up to Team Rocket.

"Battle me!" Ash yelled.

"When we battle you, we always lose," said Meowth. "We are going to run for it this time!"

Gengar flew after Team Rocket.

Jessie and James called on Arbok and Weezing.

Arbok and Weezing chased
Gengar. Gengar vanished
just in time!

Then Gengar used its Night Shade
Attack. Black beams came from its eyes.
The beams set Pikachu and Togepi free!

"Gengar, use Shadow Ball!" yelled Morty.

Gengar made a black ball of energy. It threw the Shadow Ball at Arbok and Weezing. The two Pokémon fell down.

The Shadow Ball got bigger and bigger. It rolled into Jessie, James, and Meowth.

"We are blasting off again!" Team Rocket cried.

"Thanks, Morty,"
Ash said.
"You and your
Ghost
Pokémon saved
the day!"
    "*Pikachu!*"
said Pikachu.